I Remember When ...

Alan Trussell-Cullen

Australia • Brazil • Japan • Korea • Mexico • Singapore • Spain • United Kingdom • United States

I Remember When ...

Fast Forward
Yellow Level 7

Text: Alan Trussell-Cullen
Illustrations: Julian Bruère
Editor: Kate McGough
Designer: Vonda Pestana
Series Design: James Lowe
Production Controller: Emma Hayes
Photo Research: Gillian Cardinal
Reprint: Jennifer Foo

Acknowledgements
The author and publisher would like to acknowledge permission to reproduce material from the following sources: Photographs by Australian War Memorial, p. 7/ 138692, cover, p. 1/ 003195, p. 5; Fairfax Photo Library/ Rebecca Hallas, p. 8 top; Getty Images/ Keystone/ Stringer, pp. 8 bottom,13/ The Image Bank, p. 12; State Library of Victoria, p. 11; Coo-ee Historical Picture Library, back cover, pp. 3, 4, 6, 14.

ISBN 978 0 17 012507 9
ISBN 978 0 17 012511 6 (set)

Cengage Learning Australia
Level 7, 80 Dorcas Street
South Melbourne, Victoria Australia 3205
Phone: 1300 790 853

Cengage Learning New Zealand
Unit 4B Rosedale Office Park
331 Rosedale Road, Albany, North Shore NZ 0632
Phone: 0800 449 725

For learning solutions, visit **cengage.com.au**

Printed in Australia by Ligare Pty Ltd
6 7 8 9 10 11 12 20 19 18 17 16

Evaluated in independent research by staff from the Department of Language, Literacy and Arts Education at the University of Melbourne.

I Remember When ...

Alan Trussell-Cullen

Contents

Chapter 1

THE WAR

I remember the **Second World War**. I was going to school.

DECLARATION — Page 2.

Elliott's GINGER BEER MINA WATER

The Argus.

LAWRENCE FRENCH DRY CLEANED One Quality 3'6 The Best SUITS, PLAIN FROCKS & COSTUMES

MELBOURNE, MONDAY, SEPTEMBER 4, 1939. 12 PAGES

BRITAIN AND FRANCE AT WAR WITH GERMANY

CHAMBERLAIN'S DECLARATION

"OUR CONSCIENCE IS CLEAR"

FULL SUPPORT

This is my mum, the new baby and me.

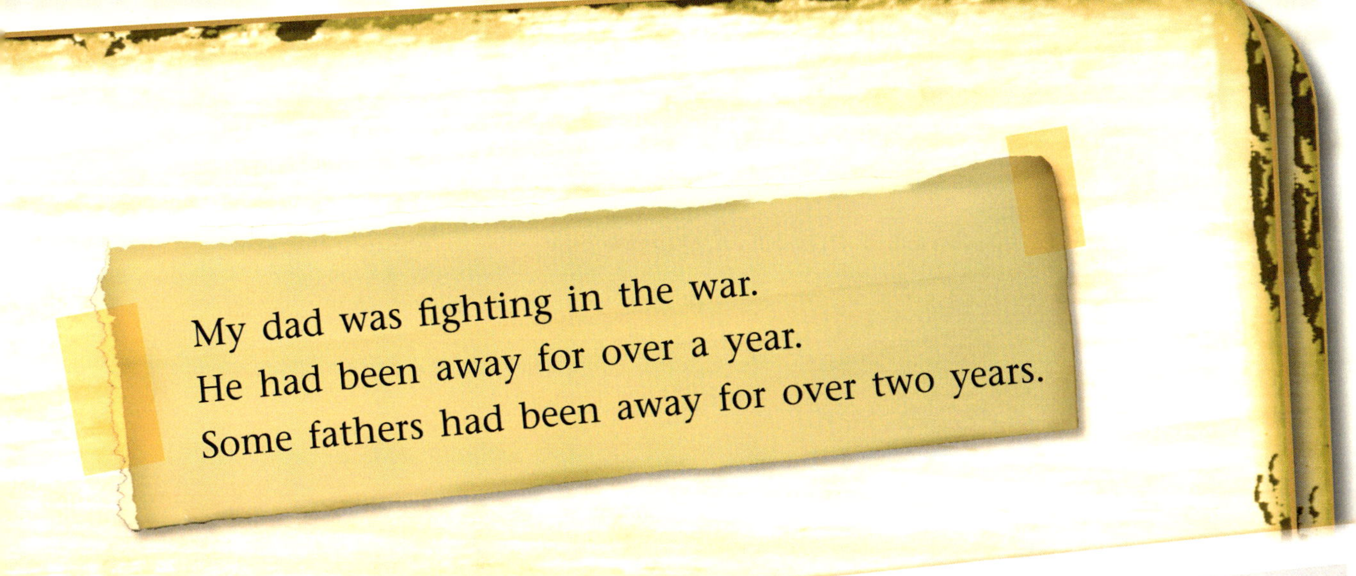

My dad was fighting in the war.
He had been away for over a year.
Some fathers had been away for over two years.

Chapter 2

LIFE WAS HARD

The war made life hard for all of us.

Mum had to have **coupons** to get food at the shops.
People had to stay in line for hours to get food for their family.

coupons

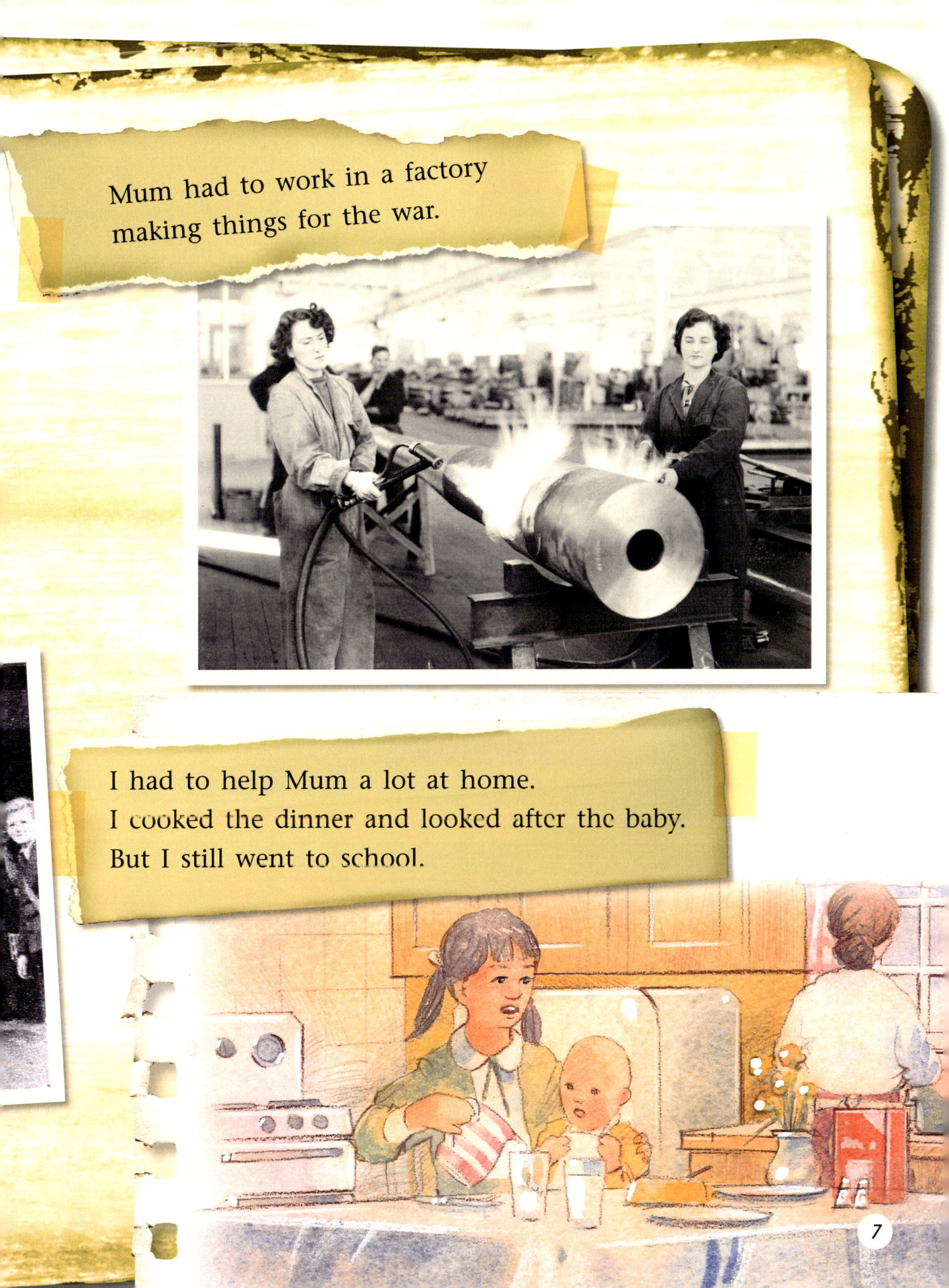

Mum had to work in a factory making things for the war.

I had to help Mum a lot at home.
I cooked the dinner and looked after the baby.
But I still went to school.

Chapter 3

GOING TO SCHOOL

This is my school.

We did our work
on little blackboards.

I walked to school,
but other children rode their bikes.
We did not have a car and there were no buses.

Chapter 4

IF THE WAR CAME TO US

Sometimes, the teacher made us sit under our desks.
She said this is what we had to do
if a plane flew over the school.

There were **trenches** behind the school.
We had to get into the trenches if a plane flew over when we were playing.

Chapter 5

THE NEWS

At night,
we sat by the radio to hear the news
about the war.

On Saturdays, we went to the movies. Before the movie, they showed **newsreels** about the war.

Chapter 6

GOOD NEWS AT LAST

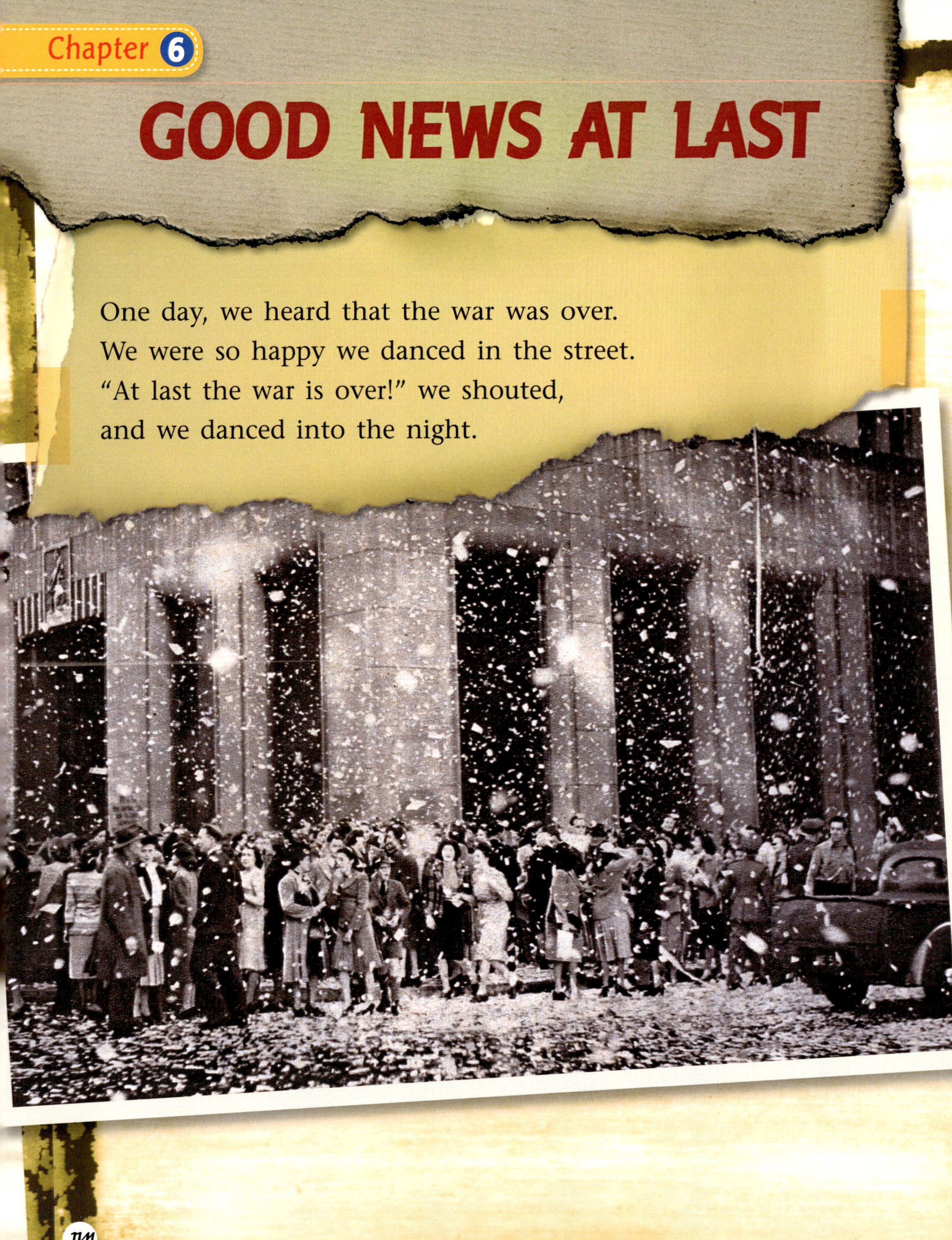

One day, we heard that the war was over.
We were so happy we danced in the street.
"At last the war is over!" we shouted,
and we danced into the night.

I remember lots of things about the war.
But, the day I like to remember again and again
is when my dad came home.

Glossary

coupons	tickets or ration cards that let you get things at the shops
Second World War	a time when people all over the world were fighting, from 1939–1945
trenches	long, thin holes dug in the ground
newsreels	short movies about the news

Index